Copyright © 2024

Jill Clarke

The moral rights of the author have been asserted.

All rights reserved.

No part of this book may be reproduced by any mechanical, photographic, or electronic process, or in the form of a phonographic recording; nor may it be stored in a retrieval system, transmitted or otherwise be copied for public or private use, other than for 'fair use' as brief quotations embodied in articles and reviews, without prior written permission of the publisher.

Contents

Foreword - 1
Dedication - 2
Introduction - 3
One Man Down - 5
Amber - 6
Archie - 8
Brownie - 10
Benji - 13
Maya & Caesar - 15
Maya - 16
Caesar - 17
Cookie - 18
Maya & Cana - 20
Maya - 22
Cana - 23
Peppa - 24
Luna - 26
Laya - 29
Hachi - 32
Junior - 34
Nezuko - 36
Polar - 39
Tilly & Toddy - 41
Tilly - 42
Toddy - 44
Walter - 46
Ghost - 49
Yoshi - 53

Contents

Coco & Pups - 55
Coco - 56
TinyTim - 59
Kai - 62
Takaani - 64
Zeus - 66
Miskia - 70
Casper - 73
Hiroshi - 81
Hoshi - 85
Darla - 88
Mya - 93
SCAR doggy Dating Site - 96
Brownie - 97
Alice - 98
Flo - 99
Kayla - 100
Penny - 101
Otis - 102
Cassie - 103
Takara & Odin - 104
Lola - 105
Louis - 106
A Rescue Dogs Plea - 107
Foster Me - 108
Acknowledgements - 109
We've Still Got you - 110

Foreword

'We've Still Got You' is the second in the series of books written on behalf of S.C.A.R–Second Chance Akita Rescue.

It is a charity close to my heart. I have been part of the Fundraising team for several years now and every penny from these books will go direct to SCAR.

As you will be aware, rescues are struggling with the demand for dogs to be helped.

It is both financially and emotionally draining–we wish we could help them all but unfortunately, that is not possible.

However, with your help, the money from each book purchased will go towards their ever-depleting funds.

So, please sit back, relax, grab a brew or a tipple, and enjoy the poems for what they are–a glimpse inside the stories of each one of these wonderful dogs.

Some will make you smile; others will bring you to tears, but please remember, these dogs are and were loved beyond belief.

Some had rocky, turbulent, abused beginnings, with help from SCAR and other charities, they have now thrived and are/were living their best lives!

I would like to thank all the Pawrents who have sent me the information on their Furbabies, I appreciate that for some it was particularly difficult. I hope you feel that I have done them justice. Happy Reading!

Dedication

This book is dedicated to Maya and Ethan, my beautiful gentle babies who are now having fun over the Rainbow Bridge.

Mummy and Daddy will miss you forever.

You took a piece of our heart, when you left.

And...

To all the other Fur Babies who are running free up there.

Have fun guys, look after each other until we meet again.

x

Introduction

We are a nation of animal lovers–we are led to believe! However, in recent times we, in rescue, have seen evidence to say differently. We have tirelessly fought to save dogs at risk of being euthanised, dogs being abused, dogs being neglected, starved, chained up, abandoned.

Is this the way a nation of dog lovers act?

The rescues all over the country and beyond are completely full to capacity, with the telephone ringing daily with other horrendous situations to deal with.

Each rescue does what it can to survive and continue to provide for these innocent souls.

Second Chance Akita Rescue is one of those organisations. Completely independent, completely reliant on volunteers and donations from the public. You add into the mix, the fact that some people are struggling to feed their children, let alone donate to charities and this is where we fundraisers step in with ideas to build the funds.

This is where I come into the equation...A little about me–

I am a Lancashire lass, just an ordinary mum, nana, wife. I work full time and volunteer for SCAR as well as for other animal charities. I have always had a love of poetry from a very young age, especially the poems that tell a story about a person, event, occasion, something that we can all relate to! I have written poems for all different situations, from births to deaths and everything in between.

I once came second in a National Poetry Competition and have had my poems published in magazines, newspapers and several books.

I am no Wordsworth, more akin to Pam Ayres!

(For those old enough to remember her).

Introduction

I would like to just finish off my introduction by saying, that just before and during the writing of these poems, I lost my two very special furbabies, Maya, my American Akita aged almost 14 years old and Ethan, my white German Shepherd at 12 years old.

It has been particularly difficult to write some of these heart-warming and heart-breaking poems, whilst I have been grieving. However, I know Maya and Ethan would want me to carry on and do what I can to raise much needed funds for SCAR.

Thank you for purchasing the second book in the series.

We really appreciate all your support and truly hope you enjoy reading the poems, written from the furbabies point of view.

(Have a good supply of tissues on hand).

With love

Jill x

One Man Down

For Paul O Grady

The Rescues are drowning, spaces non-existent,
Requests for help rehoming, daily and persistent.
And we are one man down.
The cries for help are unending,
'Put to sleep' lists extending.
And we are one man down.
We soul search each day, who do we help?
The old ones? The young ones, who sit and yelp?
And we are one man down.
Who do we turn to with our plight?
It will be a long day, a longer night.
And we are still one man down.
We've lost our ray of sunshine, we grieve so intense,
Who will be our shining light? Our moment of sense?
When we are one man down.
We ask: Who will step up? Fight the good fight?
Show the world the wrongs they can make right?
Our main man is down.
We miss you Paul, more than you know,
But we will fight, and we will show...
A rescue dog is the only way!
And the torch you worked so hard to light?
We promise to keep it burning bright.
We are one man down, but you made an impact,
We'll continue your work and will win–FACT!
Your legacy will live on, we will never lose sight,
We wish you peace, quiet, calm, we wish you goodnight!
x

Amber

Amber

My story involves a sign from the past,
A love between two, that will always last.
I came into my mummy's world,
Shortly after she lost her girl.
Meika was walking and having fun,
When suddenly Meika's life was done.
Fate dealt a blow, no-one could foresee,
This led mummy straight to me.
In 2019, Meika did depart,
Leaving my mummy with a broken heart.
Two months later, on a website,
Mummy saw my rescue plight.
I needed help, but so did she,
And so, it became, just mummy and me.
That night I slept where mummy was sitting,
Snuggled on the sofa-rather fitting!
Outside the window, a white feather was seen,
And both me and mummy knew what this means.
Meika had come to say, 'That all is ok',
Life began again for us both, that day.
She told us, that though, her job was done,
She had sent me to save our special mum.
I promise you Meika, she will always be loved,
By me here on earth, and you from above.

Archie

Archie

Mum and dad drove miles to pick me up,
I was eighteen months old, so only a pup!
I arrived from Hungary, with a wonky leg,
I will lose it one day–they should have called me peg!!
I am cheeky and stubborn, but not a bad lad.
I like to hang out, with my fabulous dad.
When he gets up, I jump in his place....
It's so funny to see the look on his face!
I'm a bit lazy, I've got it off to a tee..
I jump straight back in bed after my wee!
I share my home with two other brothers,
All of us from a different mother.
I like my space with time to reflect,
Some thinking time is what I expect.
Into the garden, I proudly stand,
Like Simba, surveying my very own land!
These are the moments I simply enjoy,
For I'm a loved, adored, wonky legged boy!

Brownie

Brownie

Brownie's the name, cheeky and soft,
I was found with my siblings living in a loft.
It wasn't very nice, we decided to move,
Aunty Vikki to the rescue, we were swiftly removed.

We all found homes, or so I am told,
But I was returned at nine months old.
There's no point on dwelling on what went before,
A new chapter begins with each open door.

Aunty Vikki to the rescue, once again,
She was the sunshine, through my rain.
I was born with a condition that affects my eyes,
But that doesn't stop me .... No surprise!

I have limited vision but can hear things for miles,
My scent work is perfect and check out my smiles!
I'm handsome and cheeky, a real cuddle bug,
There's nothing I like more than an Auntie Vikki hug.

I have learned many tricks, I can do with my paws,
The best one of all, is opening the doors!
I can take myself off for a nice gentle stroll,
But I prefer to be home, that's how I roll.

Brownie

Speaking of homes, is the one there for me?
I love Aunty Vikki, but I'm fostered you see.
I just need to feel safe, with a sofa of my own
Maybe a sister, so I don't play alone?

I have a condition but I'm handsome and bright,
All I want is pawrents to kiss me goodnight.
In return you will have all the love that you need,
From the majestic, the noble, the loyal Akita breed.

(Applications to be for the attention of 'Brave Brownie'!!)

Benji

Benji

Benji here, one of SCAR's pups, a Shepkita I will have you know!
Adopted in 2020, with plenty of time to grow.
I was only 15 months old, playful and full of fun,
I thoroughly enjoy life, and I love a good old run.

I am great with cats and small furries, in fact, with everything to be precise,
I am an all-round, perfect doggy, handsome and sweet and nice.
Mum says I have a beautiful soul, but that is down to her,
She brought me up to be a gentleman, with lots of tender care.

I'm five and half now, I'm trying to settle down.
You will always see a smile on my face, there will never be a frown….
Because I don't let life get to me, I take each day as it comes,
What is there to worry about, when by my side is mum!!

Maya and Caesar

Maya

My daddy brought me home, nanna was house proud
So, in the garden and the kitchen, I was only allowed!
Yeah right, that rule was quickly disobeyed,
And some new rules, were very swiftly made!
They were on my terms, I could go where I please,
And Nanna and Gramps were delighted to appease.
Daddy had to go away, I was feeling very sad,
But staying at Nanna and Gramps, I didn't miss dad.
They spoiled me rotten, and fed me good food,
I always smiled for them, always in a good mood.
I spent nine months with them, until daddy returned home,
I wasn't ready to leave, but daddy wanted to roam.
He was off to emigrate, and was taking me too,
I was sad to say goodbye, but it was the right thing to do.
Daddy needed me with him, he had built a new life,
Saying goodbye to Nanna and Gramps cut like a knife.
So, I made it my mission to find them a new love,
And got in touch with Caesar, who was sent from above.
He drew them in, with his sweet, tender soul,
And helped them to heal that empty hole.
We are all happy now, contented, not sad,
Caesar with Nanna and Gramps, and me with my dad!

Caesar

After Maya left, mummy and daddy felt down,
No longer were they smiling, on their face, a frown.
I came along, the timing was just right!
Out of the darkness came a shining light!
I kept them very busy, with my unpredictable tum,
They spent hundreds on food, before they found the right one.
They say Akitas are cat like, I am no different, you see–
I curved around their legs, and they fell in love with me!
I had heard on the grapevine that mummy was sad,
So, I asked Maya to send them, as my new mum and dad.
They had become smitten with the Akita breed
-Akita love is all anyone ever needs!
I set about my task, completing in record time,
Within just a few minutes, I was theirs and they were mine.
And now we live together as happy as can be,
My mummy and my daddy and little old me!!

Cookie

Cookie

At sixteen weeks old,
I was fearless and bold,
I came from the land known as SCAR!
I'd been owned for three days,
Then they gave me away,
In sixteen weeks, I had travelled so far!

Vikki welcomed me in,
For my life to begin,
And gave me love and care.
Then my mum came along,
Together we grew strong,
And I comforted my brother Bear.

Missy had now gone,
Bear was all alone,
I found my vocation in life.
To always be there,
To love and to care,
Through troubles and through strife!

I'm a bit of a minx,
So, please raise your drinks.
To welcome me into mum's arms.
At 21 weeks old,
I'm again, fearless and bold,
But this time, I will come to no harm!

Maya and Cana

Maya and Cana

Here is our tale, it's sad but true.
We wanted to share it with all of you.
We dogs can sense when someone's in need,
When their heart is broken and needs to be freed.
We met Jenny in Dec 2020,
She had suffered lots with loss a plenty.
Her parents were gone and she was lost,
Felt alone, after they had crossed.
She spoke to a friend who said come with me,
I have just the thing that will cheer you, you'll see.
That's when she met us Cana and I,
And to her sadness she said goodbye.
She began to walk us for a friend,
We enjoy every moment from start to end

Maya

I am Maya, Akita through and through,
I am six years old, cuddly too!
I am a chunky monkey, that's what they say,
But I like my food, more than I like play!
I am strong on the lead,with a high prey drive,
I once pulled a park bench, when a small dog walked by!!
I have my quirks, things I can't stand...
Walking sticks, zimmer frames, pink water bottles in hand!
These may seem strange and believe me, there's many,
But my mission in life.. to embarrass Jenny.

Cana

I'm Cana, Maya tells me I'm allowed in this book,
Though I am not an Akita, I have a different look.
I'm huge, I am strong, I am protective to the core,
I am a Czech Wolf dog...need I say more!
I was rescued from a yard at four years old,
Starved half to death, skinny and cold,
With no socialisation, in that lonely place,
I am now more than happy in my own space!
Maya can join me, other dogs?
No permission,
And to catch a squirrel is my only mission!!
(pesky little blighters)
Don't get me wrong, I do like a hug,
But trust me, you would need to wear a nose plug!
My nickname is 'Farty pants', I wonder why?
They often make Jenny and her husband cry!
I am a big fan of scrounging, out of the trash,
I smell an open lid and I'm there in a flash!
We've all helped Jenny feel better in her skin,
But she can lose it, when she shouts 'out the bin'!
We are happy and contented, that Jenny came our way,
Our walks spent with her, make a very special day

Peppa

Peppa

I was a bit of a secret, I was hidden for a few nights,
I shared a comfy bed, and finally slept tight.
Then I was discovered and my job I did begin,
To mend some broken hearts and heal the hurt within.
Mum soon called me her favourite, but she never said out loud,
My favourite was mum's new boyfriend, after all, three's a crowd!
I was as stubborn as they come, but always Miss Polite,
And still was chasing pesky foxes, up till my last night!
I decided to bow out in February Twenty Four,
I was tired, I was old, and I had done what I came here for.
I had healed their aching hearts, I had set them free,
They hurt because I left them, but they did what was best for me.

And along came Luna...

Luna

Luna

Hi, my name is Luna, I'm a husky cross Akita,
I'm not here to replace Peppa, after all, nothing could beat her.
I have settled nicely in this home, my happy little place,
With my ears that are way too big, and my silly smiling face!
I'm mending broken hearts, a little every day,
I like to see them smiling, when I begin to play.
Everybody loves me, I'm their number one,
I love food and walks and balls and toys and generally having fun!
I'm here to help them forget, their troubles and their strife,
I'm here to show them love, and to live my best life.
Peppa will never be far away, she keeps a watchful eye,
I promised her that I would love them forever, and every day I try.

Peppa

Laya

Laya

Adopted from Dogs' Trust in 2019,
I am my daddy's first dog!
Age just nine months way back then,
I was merely a sprog!

Daddy knew nothing about Akitas,
So, he did some research and a DNA.
Turned out I am pure Japanese,
(But I knew that anyway!)

He soon got to learn of my little quirks,
My in-built clock for one,
I must wake him up each time,
For my walkies to be done!

I love to play fetch for a while,
But I soon get fed up with that,
I mean, there's only so many times a lady,
Will bring that ball back!!

(You threw it.. you get it!)

He learned that I never stop shedding,
Scruffy wolf, he often calls me.
And I think he regrets the long lead,
I've killed 2 rabbits you see.

Laya

He underestimated my prey drive,
And before he could get to my head,
I had already caught the little blighters,
And left them on the ground dead.

We Akitas, are opportunists,
We see an open gate,
And take our moment of glory,
We've pegged it, you're too late!

I once went off for a wander,
Into the nearby woods.
Two hours later, I returned,
With a smile and covered in mud!

Every day is a school day,
Lessons we will remember forever,
For that is what Best Friends do,
They always learn together!

Hachi

Hachi

My name is Hachi, I'm a tom boy at heart,
When I sing it's at a high decibel.
Though I'm a tom boy, I can be a tart,
And a bit of a Jezebel!
I like to live up to my boy's name,
So, I often cock my leg,
To catch the birds is my aim,
But they always get away instead!
I have been known to pinch stuff,
I'm a bit of a tea leaf,
I once pinched a loaf, it wasn't so tough,
Yep, I'm a counter surfing thief!
Fruit is my favourite by far,
And I do like my food to chomp,
If I get it, then I'm a star,
If I don't? It's the 'Kevin and Perry' stomp!!
I like to play catch with my toys,
Well, with anything for that matter!
It's just something that I enjoy,
Especially if they make a clatter!
Though I'm one of the lads,
I do like a cuddle and a kiss.
I make a heart with my paws and pads,
Mummy and Daddy especially love this!
I'm a girl with a boy's name,
I can often throw a paddy,
To be a Tom Boy is my aim,
And to love my Mummy and Daddy!

Junior

Junior

Hi, I'm Junior, just seven years old,
Typical Akita, strong, noble and bold.
My daddy was only seventeen,
When we met and he fulfilled my dream.
He was seventeen, lonely, struggling too,
Needed a partner, to ease the blues.
I came along, and things became brighter,
Daddy showed that he was still a fighter.
Together, we are, stronger as one,
With daddy, I have so much fun.
I have given him times when he has feared,
I jumped out of his car and disappeared!
But, by a neighbour, I was thankfully caught,
I like to think, that, a lesson I taught.
What do I mean? Let me explain,
Daddy was scared he wouldn't see me again.
He panicked that he was alone once more,
But that day, I showed him, that, for sure,
No matter how dark, life may seem,
Out of the shadows, the sun will beam!
I was back by his side, in no time, you see..
That's where I belong, and forever will be.
I love and I care for all that I meet,
But my love for my daddy...you can never beat!
We are inseparable, me and my dad,
My job in this life, is to make him less sad.
And when the time comes, when I am gone,
His fighting spirit, I know, will go on.

Nezuko

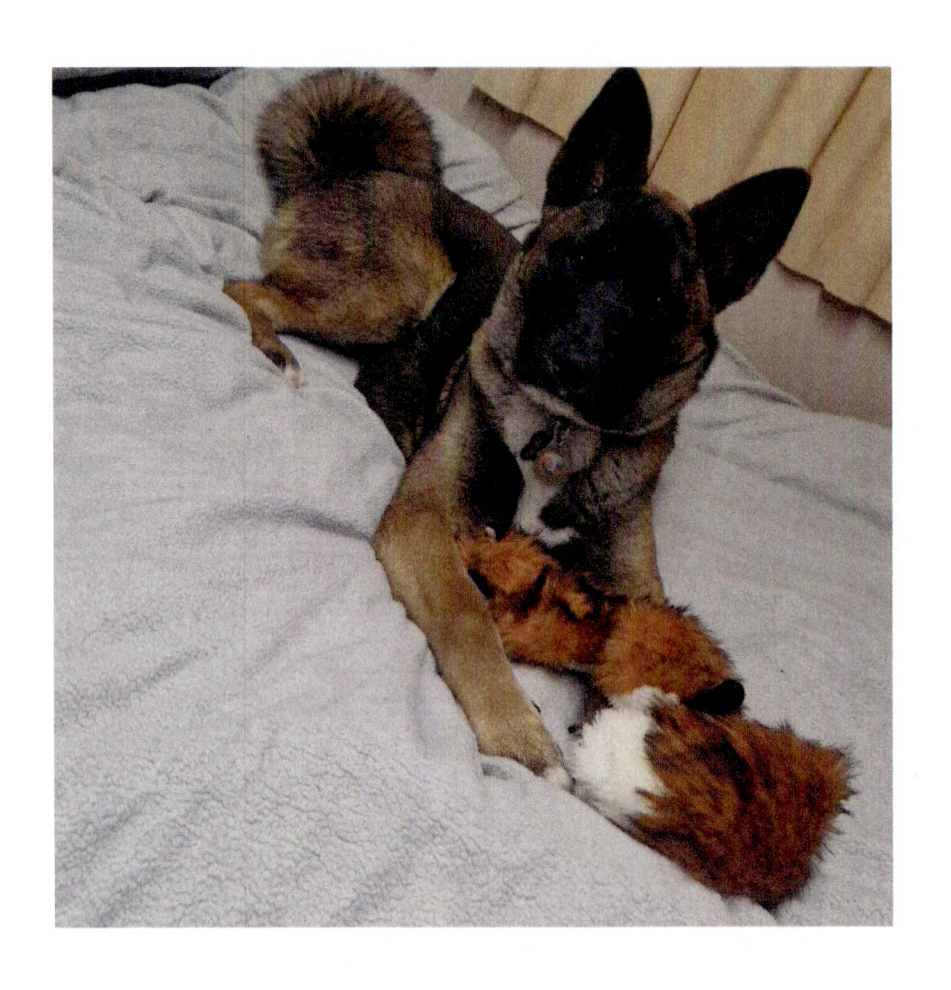

Nezuko

Nezuko's the name, playing is the game,
What else should a puppy do?
I'm an Akita cross, and I am the boss,
And now I'm nearly two!
I'm part GSD, and my dad attacked me,
Other dogs do the same!
So, I burst into verse, shout at them first,
And make sure they all know my name!
I am not too keen, on humans I mean,
It takes me a while to adjust,
But cuddles I love, so with a bit of a shove,
I eventually learn to trust.
I'm bundles of fun, according to mum,
But not when I'm out of sight,
I have a ploy, with my loudest toy,
Under the bed, at night!!
I'm a little demanding, when I am commanding,
My minions to get what I need.
I grab their hand, make a stand,
When I get what I want, then they're freed!
I'm a dog with class, and a touch of sass,
I'm a lovable cuddle bug.
I'm especially glad, when, my mum and dad,
Give me a great big hug!

Nezuko

It's my happy place, see a smile on my face,
All my worries just disappear.
With dogs that are raucous, and humans, I'm cautious,
I'm happiest when my pawrents are near.

Love you mum and dad xx

Polar

Polar

Can you guess why I'm called Polar?
Let me give you a clue,
I am white, I am brave, I am strong...
(And a bit naughty too)
I know I have my boundaries,
No matter how I plead.
I can't go in the bedrooms,
Because once, that's where I weed!
I love the stuffing in cushions,
It reminds me of the snow,
But daddy doesn't like it,
When around the room it's thrown!
I have a certain habit,
Embarrassing for some,
But before I go to the toilet,
I must run a Marathon!
(I'm just working up to it)
I really love my car rides,
They simply are the best.
And when I return home,
I lay my head to rest.
I always sleep downstairs,
To guard my special home,
Then early in the morning,
Up the stairs I roam.
I often wake dad up,
From his happy, sleepy place,
With a special morning kiss,
And my handsome smiley face!!

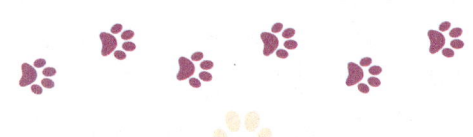

Tilly and Toddy

Tilly

Hi, my name is Tilly, and my tale is rather silly,
I was bought for a Christmas gift.
For a seven-year-old, or so I am told,
So, my training was all adrift.

Kept in a laundry room, no where to have a zoom,
No training was given to me.
No manners I had, no mum and no dad,
Given away Free, on Gumtree!

No dog food was fed, lollies and pop instead,
I needed to escape from there,
My Pawrents came along, gave me hope to carry on,
And surrounded me with care.

Manners were taught, with plenty of thought,
With love and attention too.
Big brother Brogue, saw me as a rogue,
But loved me as dog brothers do!

I live life to the full, no day is dull,
I'm stubborn but playful to boot.
I like to explore, behind walls, stairs and doors,
And I am frequently told that I'm cute.

Tilly

My Daddy's the best, I lay under his desk,
And his music I love to hear.
Have adventures when I can, in the campervan,
With mum and Dad, I no longer have fear!

Toddy

I'm Tilly's brother, from another mother,
Toddy is the name.
I also have a past, that wasn't a blast,
A drug dealers' game.

He would go out all night, I was filled with fright,
Fireworks pushed through the door.
There was no doubt, that I needed out,
I could live that life no more.

It has left me scarred, so men are barred,
I don't trust them you see.
It was all too much, I didn't like his touch,
I needed someone to look after me.

Tilly shows me care, she's my support bear,
She always leads the way.
She's quite aloof, but a bit of a goof,
With her, I feel safe to play.

Mummy is relieved, we are thick as thieves,
I know I will always be safe.
I have my own style, and a gorgeous smile,
And I'm beginning to feel more brave!

Toddy

I'm kind of coy, and a mummy's boy,
I am loved and I am respected.
I am no longer alone, with fireworks thrown,
I'm home, and I'm protected.

Walter

Walter

I am known to my friends as Pog or Wog,
But you can call me Walter the Wonder Dog!
I'm a gentle giant, with an air of calm,
I'm everyone's friend, I mean no harm.
I'm an Akita mixed with a Malamute,
With the temperament and personality to suit.
I have a job, when I'm not chilling,
It's a career that I find really thrilling.
Let me explain, where it all started,
I was a Bailiff dog, but I soon departed.
I was meant to look mean, beside my man,
But I just sat there smiling inside the van!
My vocation in life changed in a flash,
(I didn't want to force people to part with cash.)
So, my daddy adopted me, and I've never looked back,
My purpose in life was back on track!
I visit the sick, the sad and the alone,
I let them know that they are not on their own.
I put on my uniform, and look rather cool,
I cheer up the children, in hospital and school.
My dad says I calm them, these kids who are sick,
Wagging my bum is my usual trick!
I love my job, it makes me smile,
Just sitting with the kids for a short while.
Behind the scenes where only dad sees,
I'm a bit of a monkey–my dad agrees!

Walter

At 9pm I will give him a nudge,
It's Bonio time, how can he begrudge?
I don't like small furries, I could eat them in one,
But I do like to roll in some dead salmon!
I've taken myself off for a mystery tour,
Into the woods, to have an explore.
My dad, in a state, the woods he would scour,
But no need to panic, it was just half an hour!
I love my food, but there's two clear winners-
Empty yoghurt pots, and tasty chicken dinners!
Give me a soft sofa to chill for a while,
Or even better, a nice cold tile!
I'm Walter the Wonder dog, I'm gentle and kind,
A more calming influence you never will find!

Ghost

Ghost

Apparently, I lived in a 'Dogs' Home', that's what 'My' staff used to say!
I would lay quietly at the back of my room, and watch people pass by each day.
I didn't like to make too much fuss, all the other dogs at the hotel did though,
But I am an akita, quiet and dignified, my emotions I didn't like to show!
Until, one day, a lady took notice, we had met before, it was no surprise,
She volunteered at this hotel, but today she had sadness in her eyes!
She told me later, she was buying perfume, her favourite, Ghost, was its name,
But came to the 'hotel' instead, and so, that is how I got my new name.
I was fostered (I think that's what they called it), but I wasn't going anywhere, you see..
It was a special time of the year; this Christmas was all about me!
Mummy was new to Akita's, but I knew from the moment we met,
That I'd be the one to show her, exactly what she was going to get!

Ghost

I was loving and very affectionate, I brought no trouble or strife.
I wasn't keen on dogs, except one...we were like husband and wife!!
Because, I had been so silent, I didn't know that I had a voice,
Until two years later, when I barked, I jumped, no more barking..my choice!
I loved to curl up on mum's bed, with my teddy, but please take note...
I was the head of the household, so I was in control of the remote!!
I was eight when I was adopted, young, and man, could I run!
I loved to play with my football, but I grew old and my days running, were gone.
I had started to slow down, I was no longer a teen,
So, mummy helped me over the bridge, back in 2016.
Mummy, I know that you still miss me, and I know that your hearts, I stole,
But I'm running and barking over the bridge...and, I'm still in charge of the control!

Ghost

Yoshi

Yoshi

My name is Yoshi-I had a job to do,
It was a big job, and I was only two!
I'd had a few mummies, but none of them cared,
I barked at some kids, and they got scared.
I was only frustrated, no exercise, you see,
So, I asked the kids, but they didn't like me!
Along came Mummy, it all fit into place,
She gave me time to relax, gave me my space.
I wasn't keen on the 'baby thing', It made lots of mess!
But as she grew bigger, she became the best!
My job was to mend some broken hearts,
I decided that Mummy, was the place to start!
The best way to heal is to keep very busy,
So, I pinched some Carling...Mum got in a tizzy!!
I'm a bit of a monkey, but not naughty at all,
I love being in the garden with my teddy and ball.
Don't try to sing to me, that will end in disaster,
I will throw my food at you, like Charlotte, just ask her!!
I know that I'm spoiled, and very much adored,
With me around, you will never be bored!
I have healed broken hearts, though I don't like to boast.
I brought sunshine into darkness, when they lost Ghost.
But he talks to me daily, and tells me his views,
That he is watching over us, and he approves!
Mum, I've loved you deeply from the very start,
And will strive every day, to mend your broken heart!

Coco & Pups

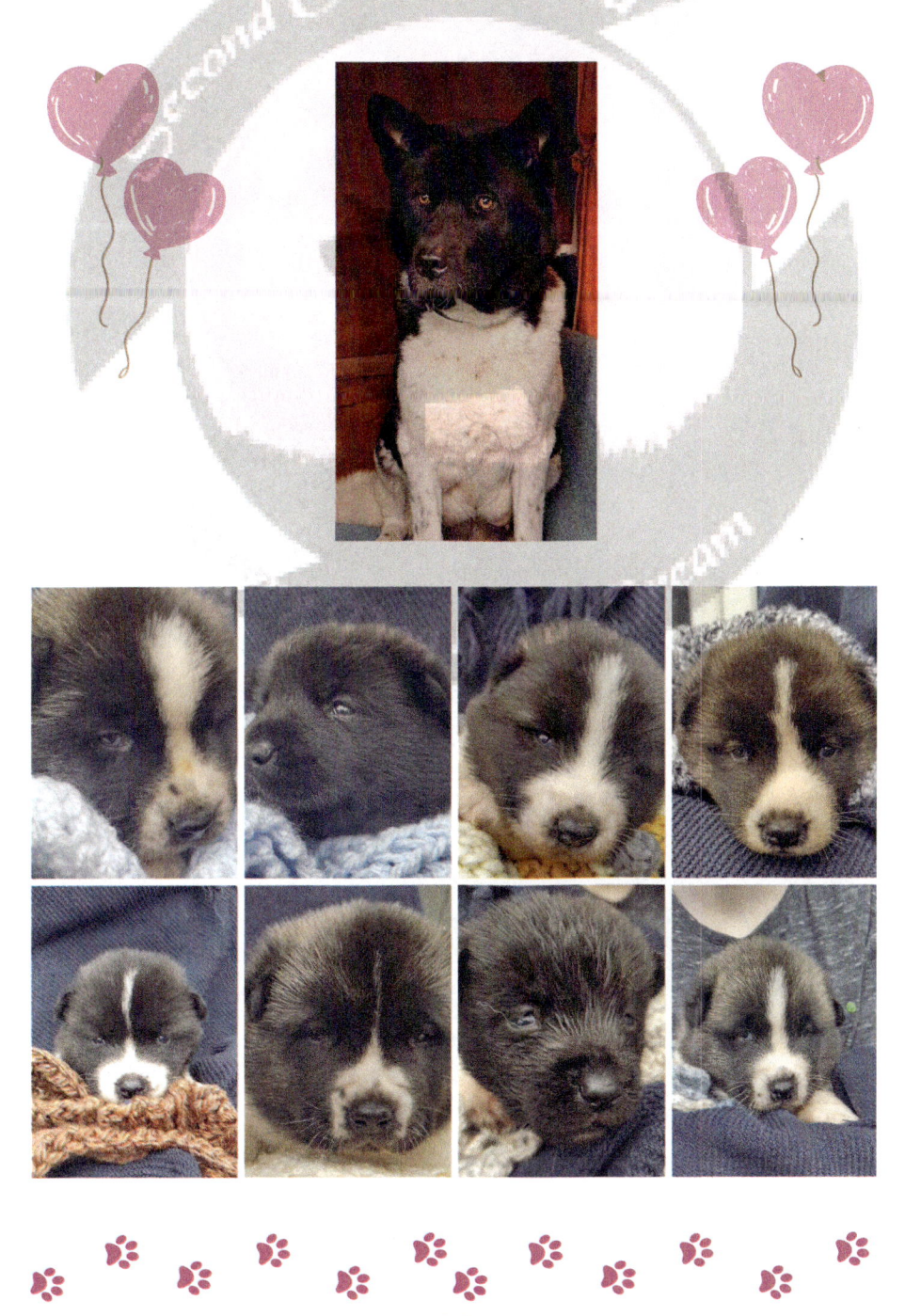

Coco

Coco

What happened? One minute I was a puppy,
The next, I was pregnant and alone,
I was scared, I was anxious, I was very bewildered,
And I desperately needed a home.

My babies were due with nowhere to go,
I had nobody to turn to for help,
Then along came SCAR and scooped me up,
With a family who would support me with whelp.

Just a few days later I was to give birth,
Eight babies successfully born.
I started late that evening time,
And they were all here by nine the next morn.

At first, I was scared in the conservatory,
I howled for attention and care,
And when the storms came in the evening,
Rebekah would always be there.

She sat comforting me for hours,
Under the table we would hide,
I no longer felt alone and scared,
I was calmer, I no longer cried.

Coco

The novelty of puppies, wore off,
Once they were weaned, I was done.
I did my dutiful mum bit,
But needed time out just on my own.

It was decided, they were getting on nicely,
My attention they no longer required.
I was more than happy with that,
For I was so weary and tired!

It was time for me to live again,
To run free, to play, to explore.
I met my Daddy, Kevin,
And I knew I would be alone no more.

Daddy and I instantly connected,
It was truly love at first sight,
Being by Daddy's side,
Will always feel just right.

We go on lots of adventures,
We explore the outside world,
He will always be my man,
And I will always be his girl.

TinyTim

TinyTim

I was the first born, Coco was my pawrent,
Seven more came, but I was the most important!
I needed special attention, I got that in abundance,
Mummy's milk was not enough, so she was made redundant!
I had to be hand fed, I had ill thrift which means –
I lost weight rapidly; I was small and very lean.
My adopted family, simply wouldn't give up,
They fought hard to keep me alive, to be a chunky pup.
I began to gain weight, on the formula they would feed,
But I preferred to bathe in it, its what every dog needs!
Cleopatra said its good for you, it sets your skin free -

(What's good for Cleopatra, is certainly good for me!!)

Then came the sad day that I felt unwell again,
Something strange happened, I collapsed and then,
A fit I had right there and then, it shook me to the core,
My pawrents scooped me up and rushed out of the door.
Another trip to the vets, to see what was occurring,
Mum and dad researched lots; nothing was deterring.
I was put on special meds, in hope to stop the seizure,
Sadly, they have happened again, but I'm a great believer.
I've always been tenacious, the first to try things out,
I led the way with my siblings, to show what grass was all about.

TinyTim

Mummy calls me a Trailblazer, I never will give up,
For I am just starting out, at eight months old, a pup!
Nothing will keep me down, I'm always on the go,
Playing with my sister Poppy, sleeping with Max, my Bro.
I have a fighting spirit, it comes from deep within,
Mummy says I am Tremendous, to others I'm TinyTim.

Kai

Kai

Mummy says, every day, I'm a foody through and through,

Yorkshire Puds are just too good, (I sometimes pinch them too!)
I often cry and give a big sigh, when daddy leaves the room,

The hosepipe? Scary! The hoover? I'm wary, why can't they use a broom?
I like walks in the wood, and playing tug, with Neeka, my big Sis!
We wrestle and play, till she says 'no way'! Then I give her a kiss!
I won't pretend – she's my best friend, we will never be apart,

My family I picked, and that's where I'll stick, I truly stole their heart.
Through fields I run, like Coco, my mum, my spirit is young and free,
On holidays, I go, in a caravan, you know, all the wildlife I like to see.
I would splash and play, in water all day, it simply is the best,

Kai is the name, playing is the game, now I'm off to have a rest!

"See ya, don't wanna be ya!!"

Takaani

Takaani

I was born on the day, Miskia passed, I was born into SCAR's care,
Saved from the pound and fostered, my story I would like to share.
I was the only one in the litter with a long fluffy mane,
Chunky, handsome, cheeky, with ears no one can tame!
They have never quite stood up, but people say that's cute,
To be honest, I quite like them, so I won't be the one to refute!
I've been brought up with a cat, his mannerisms I have adopted,
You will find me on the chair arm, for his stance, I have opted!
I like to watch the neighbours, see what they are doing,
Make sure that all is calm, and there's no trouble brewing!!
When visitors arrive, I let them know they are invited,
But I often piddle on the floor, when I get too excited!
My favourite time of the day, Is when, as quiet as a mouse,
I stroll along with mum and dad, Into the Doghouse!!
I'm quite a laid-back dude, often in a chilled-out state,
And when mummy gets her uniform on, I climb into my crate.
But now I have discovered that I can climb the stairs,
I suspect there's more mischief, That I can get up to, up there!

(So, mum and dad, beware!)

Zeus

Zeus

I was born in 2023, into SCAR's care,
Along with seven siblings, my mum was Coco Bear.
My new mummy called me Zeus, it was a fitting name,
With a name like that, when I grow up, I would have the fame.
But that day never came!

I was cheeky and mischievous, sneaky and loved my walks,
I could hold conversations with my endless talks!
I was vocal, not the quiet one, my mum was led to believe,
Once I'd found my feet at home, there was nothing I couldn't achieve!
But now my family grieve.

I would give kisses freely, a gigolo of sorts,
But my favourite thing of all was always, the 'zoomie' sports!
If the back door was open, "game on" was my cry,
I would gear myself up and out in the garden I'd fly.
But now I'm flying high.

I was the perfect sous chef, when mum began to cook,
I'd lay down on the kitchen floor and give the 'hungry' look!
My favourite part of the kitchen was definitely, the fridge,
It held the cosseted cheese.. and I was allowed a smidge!
But now, I'm on the Rainbow Bridge.

Zeus

I was only six months old, a baby, starting out,
There were plenty of things left for me to learn about.
The time on Earth that I spent, I really don't regret,
I know that when I left, many people were upset.
But please try not to fret

For now, I'm running free, in fields made of cheese,
I have no lead upon me, I can run between the trees.
I sit and watch the sunset, from way upon high,
And often question to myself, was it my turn to die?
But I never sigh.
And I know why….
Because mum, I'm happy up here, watching you from the sky!
Please don't cry. xx

Zeus

Forever in our Hearts

Miskia

Miskia

I was a very pretty girl, with a gentle caring soul,
I helped my mummy lots, in my supporting role.
Mummy got quite poorly, I was always by her side,
I know I helped her through it, and I did it with such pride.

Mummy picked me up, on New Years Day 2010,
I was just a few weeks old way back then,
I was always mummy's baby, this I had no doubt,
Whatever mummy's issues – I would always work them out!

I loved everybody, and everybody loved me,
My best friend, apart from mum, was my favourite Pony.
I also loved cats, four of them in all,
We loved to sleep together, all tucked up in a ball.

I treated them like babies, I never became a mum
Lots of phantom pregnancies, but no pups of my own.
I loved going to the pub, even had my own dish!
The only thing missing? A walk home with chips and fish!

I crossed the Rainbow Bridge in October 2023,
Quietly in my garden, mummy, daddy and me.
I felt so happy knowing they were with me that day,
And I want to say to mummy, that 'I'm doing ok'.

Miskia

Casper

Casper

Hi, I am Casper, I came from the pound,
I had no family, there was no one around.
I pulled like a train, and couldn't sit still,
I was a licker, a heartbreaker, with an iron will.
SCAR picked me up, and my life became sweet,
With Aunty Alison, to look after me and Uncle Piet.
I had poorly eyes, and needed an op,
I was supposed to rest after.. but I didn't stop!
Life was too short, I danced in the sun,
I guess I knew my life, would be a short one.
Aunty Alison took me to places I'd see-
All the wonderous sights there ever could be!
We walked for hours, day after day,
She never gave up; she allowed me to play.
The kennel became empty, and I was alone,
Desperate for a human to call my own.
So, we embarked on journeys, just she and I,
And sat on rocks and stared at the sky.
We talked for hours, day and night,
About how we could put the world to right.
She taught me a lot, to be calm and be still,
But to never give up my iron will!
We had picnics and ice cream, what a delight,
I was the happiest boy; I was shining bright!
The kennels got busy, and more dogs appeared,
I showed them the way, to be calm with no fear.

Casper

I loved my toys, throwing balls in the air,
I ran around playing without any care.
Then one day my tummy became very sore
Worse than a tummy ache I felt before.
Uncle Piet and Aunty Alison, rushed to my side,
I could hear Aunty Alison, oh how she cried.
I wanted to lick her and show her my love,
But now I can show her, from the bridge up above.
It was bloat that claimed me, but my life was fun,
I had no home as such, but I had a mum.
Mummy Alison, I know you now feel bereft,
You were there when I arrived, and there when I left.
No need to cry, there's plenty to do,
I'm teaching the dogs here, to be calm too!
I am giving them love and sharing my toys,
I'm splashing in pools, with the good girls and boys.
I will never forget, our time together,
So, don't cry for me, I will love you forever.

Casper

Hiroshi

Hiroshi

I speak to you from the Rainbow Bridge, beyond the silver clouds.
Where I can run, free from pain, amongst the doggy crowds.
I'm happy way up high, don't be sad that, here I came.
I watch mum and dad battle, with Demon dog, to tame!
It often makes me smile, I sent him there you see,
They were broken hearted from the day that they lost me.
Daddy says I was a special boy, majestic, rare and strong,
Brave and noble and gentle, I could do no wrong!
I protected my loved ones daily, they rescued me from the chain,
Tied to a gate in Poland, Dad ensured it wouldn't happen again.
I was brought to breed in the UK, but put into retirement,
My ears never did stand up, so, I was surplus to requirements.
I was rescued by the best family any dog could ever wish for,
I had my pup sister to play with, and my hooman sister I adored.
At first, I was very anxious, the curtains I would hide behind,
Mummy and Daddy were patient, they really didn't mind.
I soon began to realise that hiding was very rude.
I came out from behind the curtains – after all, there was food!
Food was my arch nemesis; I could never resist a snack!
I was beginning to feel comfortable, part of my own pack.
I loved to go on walks, to play and have some fun,
But if my lead wasn't on fast enough, I would simply nip their bum!!
(The clock was ticking!!)

Hiroshi

I remember one day the snow came, oh my, that day was brill!
Having 'zoomies' in the snow, was such an exciting thrill!
Unfortunately, not for dad, in my excitement I knocked him down,
Then pinched the hat and scarves, and promptly ran around!!
(I loved that day, Daddy)

I could talk about my memories, forever and a day
I will never forget my time on Earth, those memories will stay.
My Daddy says he was lucky, but I am the lucky one.
To have spent my life with my family, dancing in the sun.
We had so many adventures, each single one I treasure,
The destination didn't matter, the journey was the pleasure.
I grew old and I grew poorly, I knew my end was nigh,
But I made sure to wake them up, just to say Goodbye.
I didn't want to leave you mum and dad, I didn't want to see you cry,
That's why I am here to tell you, that I watch you from the sky.
Please remember all I taught you; I know that you know how,
Drink from all the hose pipes, live in the moment, in the now.
Don't remember me with tears, remember me with love,
I will always be your 'miracle boy', protecting from above.

**Love you lots, Mummy and Daddy,
Thank you for everything x**

Hiroshi

Hoshi

Hoshi

I ran rings around all I knew, I had not a care!
I was white as the driven snow, known as Polar Bear!
I was quite unruly, everyone knew my name,
I was naughty as a puppy, and so, I had fame.
As time then went on, with all that I was trained,
I soon became an Angel, and friendliness I gained.
I stood so very proud, for all my minions to see,
There was no one more regal-than Hoshi-that's me!
My toys were just my babies, I cuddled them each day,
But I feared Leo the turtle, and anyone with a spray!
I was quite stubborn, mum's patience I would test,
When I would just plonk down, on a walk, for a rest!
I loved my beauty sleep, often curled up with my toys,
And now I'm on the rainbow bridge, being the best boy!
I know your house feels empty mum, I know you grieve me still,
But I loved you for all my life, And I always will.

Hoshi

Darla

Darla

I'm not going to sing my praises,
That just isn't my way,
But I'd like to tell you a story,
How I helped my daddy each day…

We met when he was happy,
With a wife, some children, a home.
All was going along nicely,
Until she upped and left him alone.
But I was by his side.
He was sad, and feeling lost,
But I showed him the light.
We sat in silence often,
Others, we spoke all night.
I was always by his side.
Grandma became poorly,
So, we both moved in with her,
We worked together, as always,
To Grandma we gave such care.
And then she was no longer there.
Daddy was broken hearted,
I healed his pain once more.
I taught him that each chapter that ends,
Another will open a door.
I was always there for him.

Darla

I became so old and so frail,
Every month at the age of fourteen,
I would take a trip for medicine,
To the vets, where they called me 'Queen'.
It helped a little
Each time I would be injected,
With something to ease the pain.
But the pain would return,
Again, and again and again.
My job here was done.
One day on our way to the vets,
I knew my day had come.
I didn't want to say goodbye,
But my pain was no longer numb.
You did what was right Daddy.
I didn't need to speak a word,
It only took one look.
And daddy knew just what to do,
Time for a new chapter in the book.
You've got this Daddy.
He says I saved his life,
For me, I'm not too sure.
But I knew that he was stronger,
And didn't need his rock anymore.
It's your chapter now, Daddy.

Darla

So, I left this world at peace,
Knowing my role was complete,
It's time to fight on Daddy,
Don't give in to defeat.
I will never leave your side!

Darla

Mya

Mya

Well, hello there, hiya, my name is Mya,
I was found in the middle of nowhere!
I was poorly, docs said, from me had been bred,
I needed someone to care.
My mummy came, gave me my name,
Administered some CBD.
She loved and she cared, was always there,
She really did look after me.
Pain relief she would seek, as they gave me six weeks,
But I was to prove them wrong,
With good food to eat, and the occasional treat,
I showed them I was 'Akita' strong!
I was eleven years old and mummy was told,
That surgery was not an option.
Meds were out, they would hold no clout,
So it was mummy's CBD concoction!!
A walk every day, the occasional play,
A bit of mischief didn't go amiss!
Six months I would last, and boy, what a blast,
With mummy my life was bliss.
Up here, I play, and eat all day,
Up here I'm no longer in pain.
So, thank you to mum, for all that you've done,
My Angel wings, I have now gained.

Love you lots Mummy xx

Mya

S.C.A.R. Doggy Dating Site

We present to you, some of S.C.A.R's 'single' doggies.
Please take a look at their profiles and feel free to apply.
They are all ready and eager to meet you!!
They don't ask for much, just a warm sofa, good food, walks
and cuddles. You will get lots of love in return!

Brownie

Hi, I'm Brownie, a very special Bear,
I have an eye condition, but I don't really care.
I have two poems in this book, I'm important you see,
Just apply for 'Brave Brownie' and leave the rest to me!!

Alice

I'm a two-year-old pocket rocket,
As sweet as sugar and spice,
A family with kids over ten,
Would be very nice!

Flo

Hi, I'm Flo a little Gem, my foster pawrents say,
My favourite thing to do, is to fetch a ball and play.
I'm looking for that special home, with kids over ten,
Someone to love and spoil me and make me feel good again.

Kayla

My name is Kayla, I'm new to the gang,
I was rescued from the dreaded pound.
But I've been a star, so far in SCAR,
A new family for me, I'd like found!

Penny

Penny is my name, and I'm really rather stressed,
I don't like these kennels, I'm not impressed.
I am trying to stay calm, but find it hard to do,
I want my own family, could that be you?

Otis

I'm a funny fella and only two years old,
I have a very long tongue–so I am told.
My helicopter tail simply won't desist,
So come on folks, apply for me–how could you resist!!

Cassie

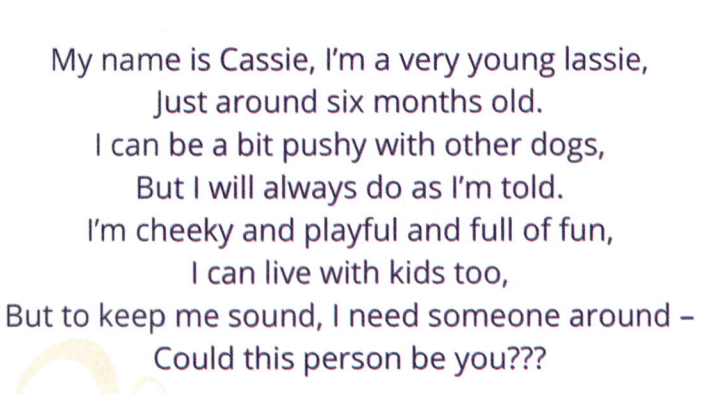

My name is Cassie, I'm a very young lassie,
Just around six months old.
I can be a bit pushy with other dogs,
But I will always do as I'm told.
I'm cheeky and playful and full of fun,
I can live with kids too,
But to keep me sound, I need someone around –
Could this person be you???

Takara and Odin

We come as a pair, mother and son,
So please don't ask if you can just take one.
We are bonded together and will cry if apart,
We need someone special to mend our hearts.
We are friendly and sweet, but pull like a train,
So, manners will need teaching again!
No children under teenage years,
And no other dogs, or there will be tears!

Lola

My name is Lola, I was a showgirl,
Only kidding, I was a stray!!
I like to give out cuddles –
I don't worry about PDA!
I'm a happy go lucky girl,
One without a care,
Looking for my family –
Is there anybody there??

Louis

I'm Louis, I have a skin condition,
But it does not slow me down,
I love to play with my toys,
And act like the class clown!
My life has been a little cruel,
Before I came to SCAR,
I'm now looking for a special person,
I wonder where they are?
I don't let my condition,
Dictate who I am,
So, please open your heart,
And let me be your man!!

A Rescue Dogs Plea

Please be patient –I need you to be
Everything around is new to me!
It will take a while for me to adjust,
To learn to love and learn to trust.
I may misbehave – boundaries crossed.
I may pretend that I am the boss!
I may not lay on my nice new bed,
But hide behind the sofa instead.
I may not eat what you supply,
I may not look you in the eye.
Don't be alarmed, please don't give up,
I may look nervous, inside I'm a pup!
When I'm comfortable – and it will take time!
I'll be yours forever, and you will be mine!
I promise soon it will be worthwhile,
Upon my face will be a smile!
Then within my heart you'll always be
The main focus for my eternity.
And if you feel it's all too much,
My support will be there - so get in touch!
They helped me when I needed care,
And I know for you, they will be there!
Before I finish I just want to say,
Thank you for giving me this **'Gotcha' day!**
I won't forget what you have done …
For making me your number one!!
x

Foster Me

I'm a little bit stinky, I'm a little bit sore,
Foster me – no-one could love you more!
I'm a little bit sad, I'm a little bit scared,
Foster me and I will know that you care!
I'm a little bit lonely, I'm a little bit sick,
Foster me and all my boxes you'll tick!
I'm a little bit anxious, I'm a little unsure,
Hoomans have let me down before!
You're a little bit scared of what to expect,
I'll bring fun, laughter, love, and respect!
It will take a while – we'll get there together,
You may even fail and adopt me forever!
But rest assured, if you foster me,
Feel happy that you helped just one doggy.
I just need time, some comfort and care,
And reassurance that you will be there.
To help me get back on my four feet,
Keep me safe, while this sadness, I defeat.
Fostering will help me enjoy better days,
And forget the past and all its sad ways.
I promise, our time, be it short or long,
Will heal my heart and right the wrongs.
Foster me please and you will not regret,
Foster me – I promise, I will never forget!
x

Acknowledgements

Tincie Hill – for planting the seed and her unwavering support.

Su 'The Face' Pilkington – For her talent on navigating all things Techy!

Beyond the Dawn Digital Ltd – For the loan of Su.

SCAR – For allowing me to flex my artistic license for the Dogs' benefits. (Secondchanceakitarescue.co.uk)

The Pawrents – For opening their hearts and their homes to the Woofers and giving them a Second Chance.

Maya, for introducing me to the Akita Clan 12 years ago

And most importantly the Woofers – For giving me the inspiration to write these poems.

Thank you to each and every one of you!

(All the proceed from the sale of this book go directly to Second Chance Akita Rescue UK

Second Chance Akita Rescue

Ev'ry Dog has a Dream

'We've Still Got You!'

We're tired, we're frustrated, we're angry, we're broken,
Just a few of the words, from a Rescue, that's spoken.
It's relentless, it's hard, overwhelming, heart breaking,
There's no room, no money, but we'll find space, we'll take him!

We'll take your dog you've abandoned, neglected,
We'll clean the wounds so badly infected.
We'll nurse him better, give him a reason to live,
We'll show him the respect, that you couldn't give.

We'll hold him close, give him a warm bed,
Take him on long walks, ensure he is fed.
We'll find him the home, that surrounds him with love,
For he is an angel, sent from above.

Welcome my boy, you're safe in rescue,
For we are S.C.A.R., and **'We've Still got you'**!

Printed in Great Britain
by Amazon